PAPA'S
LATKES

STORY AND PICTURES BY
Jane Breskin Zalben

HENRY HOLT AND COMPANY
New York

Henry Holt and Company, Inc., *Publishers since 1866*
115 West 18th Street, New York, New York 10011

Henry Holt is a registered trademark of Henry Holt and Company, Inc.

Published in Canada by Fitzhenry & Whiteside Ltd.,
195 Allstate Parkway, Markham, Ontario L3R 4T8.

Library of Congress Cataloging-in-Publication Data
Zalben, Jane Breskin.
Papa's latkes: story and pictures/ by Jane Breskin Zalben.
Summary: Papa and the little bears make latkes for Chanukah.
Includes the song "O Chanukah" and a recipe for making latkes.
[1. Chanukah—Fiction. 2. Cookery—Fiction. 3. Jews—Fiction.
4. Bears—Fiction.] I. Title. PZ7.Z254 Pap 1993 E—dc20 93-37986
ISBN 0-8050-4634-8

First published as a mini novelty edition in 1994 by Henry Holt and Company, Inc.
This edition published in 1996 by Henry Holt and Company, Inc.
Typography by Jane Breskin Zalben.
The text type was set in Caslon 540.
The art was done with a 000 brush using watercolors on imported Italian paper.
Printed in the United States of America on acid-free paper. ∞

1 3 5 7 9 10 8 6 4 2

To Steven—
our very own Papa,
who makes the best blackened latkes

ama made the best
potato pancakes in the whole town.
"This Chanukah," she said, "I don't
feel like making latkes." So Papa
said, "Let's have a latke contest!"
Beni flipped his latke in the air.
And it landed on Sara's head.

Rosie added extra potatoes.
Her latkes were lumpy.

Max's were so oily, they slipped
right off the plate into Leo.

Leo made his into strange shapes.

No one would eat them.

Blossom's were too brown.
Goldie's were too raw.

Molly's were too large.
Sam's were too small.

Finally, Papa cried, "Step aside."
He peeled and grated and mixed the
potatoes until the batter was smooth.
Everyone watched carefully. He made
pancake after pancake after pancake.
They were stacked so high, Papa and
Mama nearly disappeared.

When Papa was done, the whole family helped carry all the latkes to the table. Mama put a dab of fresh sour cream and homemade applesauce next to each one.
They weren't too dark.
They weren't too light.
All agreed, "These are perfectly round, and just right. Let's celebrate!"

Candles were lit in the menorah.
Mama's favorite song, "O Chanukah!"
was sung many times. Everyone danced,
played dreidel, and opened presents.

For the first night of Chanukah,
each cousin got a bag of chocolate
gelt, and a new, shiny frying pan.
"To make your own latkes," Papa said,

"for all eight nights."
"But yours are the best!" Beni shouted.
"Yours will be too!" Papa smiled.
"I'll teach you how tomorrow."

Papa gave everyone a kiss. So did Mama. "Now go to sleep," they both whispered. And the children did, with their tummies stuffed with Papa's latkes.

O Chanukah

Arranged by Alexander Zalben

O Cha-nu-kah, O Cha-nu-kah, come light the Me-no-rah._
Oy Cha-nu-koh, oy Cha-nu-koh, a yom-tov a shay-ner, a

Let's all have a par-ty, we'll all dance the ho-rah.
lus-stig-er, a fray-lich-er, nit-du noch a zoi-ner,

Gath-er 'round the ta-ble; you'll get a treat. Shi-ny tops to play with,
al-le nacht in drayd-lech shpie-len_ mir, zi-dig hay se lat-kes

pan - cakes to eat. And while we are play - ing, the
est un a shir. Ge - shvin - der tsint kin - der die

can - dles are burn - ing___ low. One for each night they___
din - in - ke lich - te - lach un. Zugt al ha - ni - sim loibt

shed a sweet light, to re - mind us of days long a - go.
gott far die ni - sim un kumt gi - cher tant - zen in kon.

Papa's Latkes

4-5 large potatoes   1/4 cup matzoh meal
1 medium onion   salt and pepper
2 large eggs   vegetable oil

1. Peel potatoes, wash in cold water, grate finely.
2. Grate onion on larger side of grater.
3. Beat 2 eggs and add to mixture.
4. Blend in matzoh meal, and salt and pepper to taste with other ingredients.
5. Heat 1″ layer of vegetable oil in large frying pan. Drop in 1 heaping tablespoon of mixture for each latke, and when it sizzles turn over until it's crisp and golden.
6. Drain on paper towels.
7. Serve with sour cream or applesauce.

Papa sometimes likes to add parsley, dill, apples, raisins, cinnamon—or even cayenne pepper—to his latkes recipe.

Serves about 6, depending on their appetites